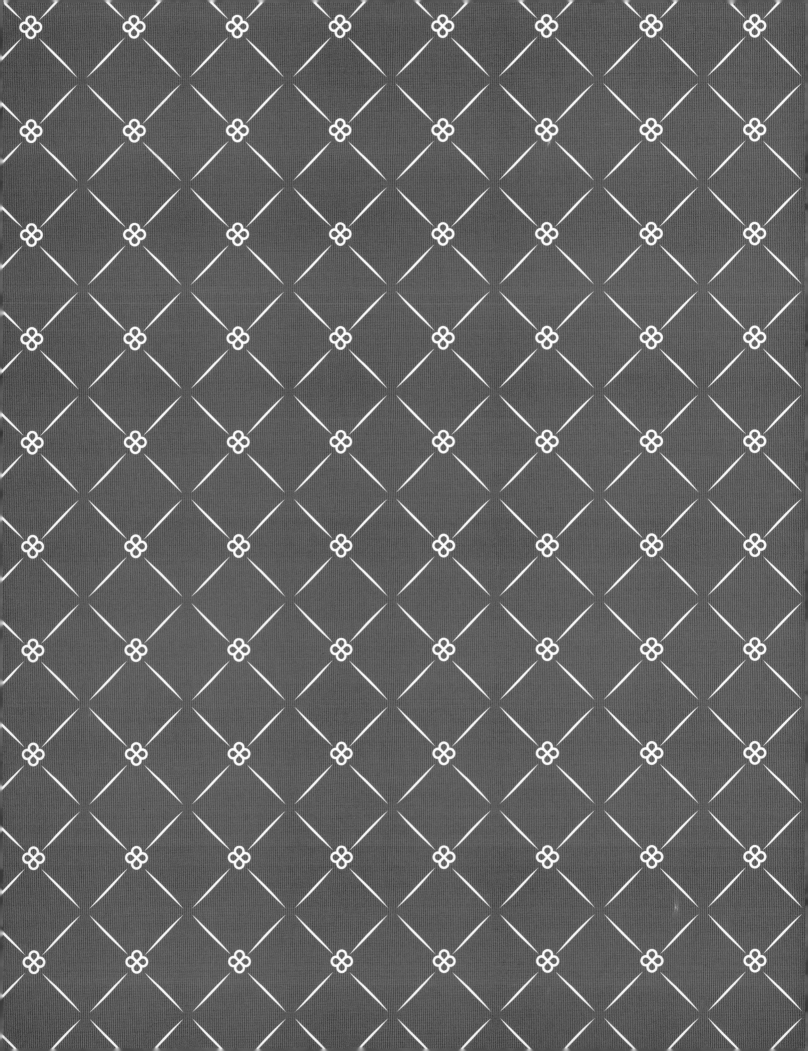

This book belongs to

_____

_____

This edition published by Parragon Books Ltd in 2017

Parragon Books Ltd
Chartist House
15–17 Trim Street
Bath BA1 1HA, UK
www.parragon.com

ISBN 978-1-4748-6914-0

Printed in China

DISNEY MOVIE COLLECTION
A SPECIAL DISNEY STORYBOOK SERIES

BEAUTY
AND THE
BEAST

PaRragon
Bath • New York • Cologne • Melbourne • Delhi
Hong Kong • Shenzhen • Singapore

Once upon a time, a spoiled, selfish prince lived in a castle in the forest. One night, an old beggar woman offered the prince a rose in return for shelter. Repulsed by her appearance, the unkind prince turned her away.

Suddenly, the old woman turned into an enchantress. She transformed the prince into a beast and placed a spell on the entire castle. To break the spell, the prince must learn to love – and be loved in return – before the last rose petal fell. Otherwise, he would remain a beast forever.

Not far away, a young woman named Belle
lived in a small village. She dreamed of a more
exciting life and wanted adventures like the ones
in her favourite books.

Belle was very beautiful and had long been admired by Gaston, the most handsome and vain man in the village.

Gaston was certain that Belle would feel lucky to marry him. But Belle thought Gaston was rude and bad-mannered – and he didn't understand her love of books.

Belle returned home to find her father, Maurice, surrounded by pieces of his latest invention.

"I'll never get this bone-headed contraption to work!" said Maurice.

"Yes, you will," said Belle. "And you'll win first prize at the fair tomorrow."

With Belle's encouragement, Maurice quickly finished his automatic wood chopper. Then he loaded it onto a wagon and set out with his horse, Phillipe, for the fair.

Belle knew the villagers thought Maurice was odd, but he was her father and she always believed in him.

As evening fell, Maurice realized he had taken a wrong turn. He was lost, deep in the forest.

When wolves howled nearby, Phillipe threw Maurice off and bolted. The snarling wolves cornered Maurice in front of a huge gate. He banged on the gate until it opened, then gratefully stumbled inside.

Maurice crept into the enormous castle
that lay beyond the gate. Before long,
he heard voices whispering. He nervously
picked up a candlestick to light his way.

"Hello!" said the candlestick.
Maurice couldn't believe his ears!
All of a sudden, the castle seemed full
of enchanted objects that could move
and talk.

The candlestick, whose name was Lumiere, led Maurice
to a comfortable chair in front of a warm fire.

Suddenly, a terrifying beast stormed into the room.
"So you've come to stare?" the Beast growled.

"I meant no harm," Maurice stammered. "I needed
a place to stay."

"I'll give you a place to stay," the Beast snarled.
Then he locked Maurice in the dungeon.

Meanwhile, Gaston arrived at Belle's cottage. He announced that Belle's dreams were about to come true. He had made all of the preparations and planned for them to marry that very day!

"I'm very sorry, Gaston, but I don't deserve you," Belle replied.

Furious, Gaston left the house, "I'll have Belle for my wife, make no mistake about that!" he shouted.

Just then, a frightened Phillipe galloped into the yard.
"What happened?" asked Belle. "Where's Papa?
You have to take me to him!"
So Phillipe led Belle in the direction of the castle.

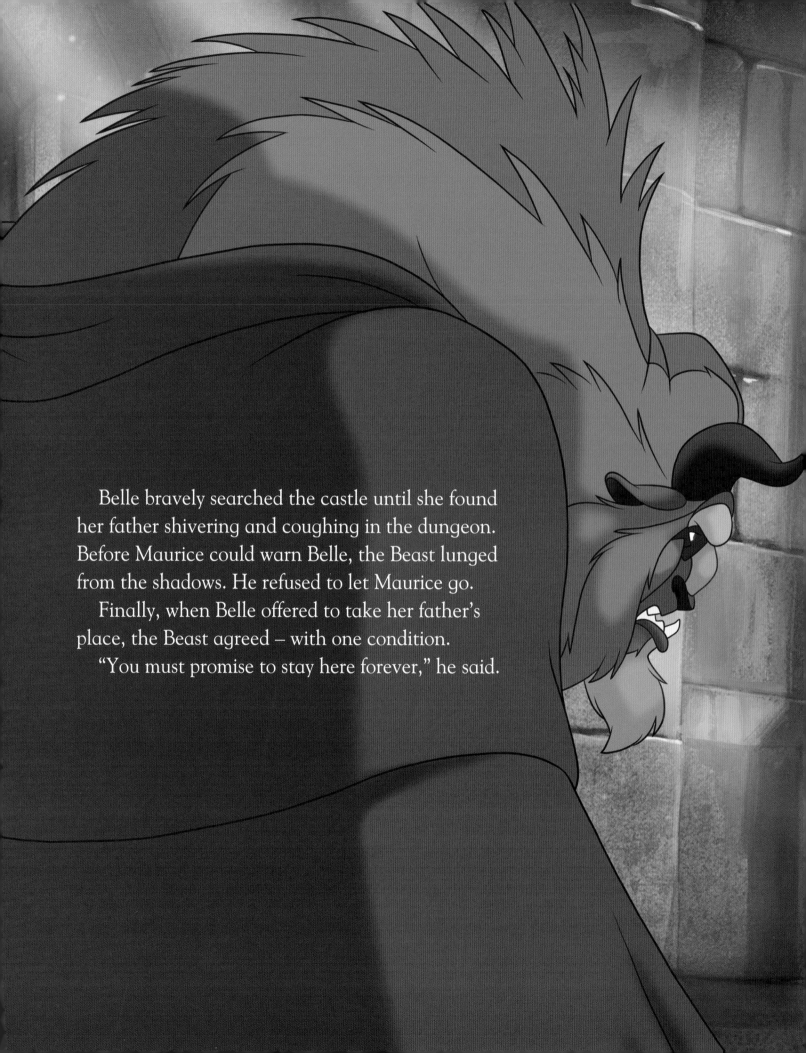

Belle bravely searched the castle until she found her father shivering and coughing in the dungeon. Before Maurice could warn Belle, the Beast lunged from the shadows. He refused to let Maurice go.

Finally, when Belle offered to take her father's place, the Beast agreed – with one condition.

"You must promise to stay here forever," he said.

Belle refused to join the Beast for dinner. Instead, she waited until it was late, then crept down to the kitchen where she met some of the castle's enchanted servants, including a teapot called Mrs Pott, her son, Chip, and a clock named Cogsworth.

To Belle's delight, the staff treated her to a magnificent feast with singing and dancing. They were thrilled to finally have a guest!

After dinner, Belle wanted to explore
the castle. The Beast had forbidden her to go into
the west wing but Belle was curious. Although Cogsworth
and Lumiere tried to discourage her, Belle slipped away from
them and went up the stairs.

Belle peered into a dark room and gasped. Broken furniture and
mirrors lay scattered as if someone had torn everything apart in a rage.
Then Belle saw a rose glowing under a glass dome. She noticed that
several petals had fallen off. Entranced by its beauty, Belle reached out.

But before Belle could touch the rose, the Beast burst into the room.

"I warned you never to come here!" he bellowed. "Do you know what you could have done? Get out!"

Terrified, Belle ran from the castle. "Promise or no promise, I can't stay here another minute!" she cried.

She climbed onto Phillipe, who was waiting outside, and raced into the forest. Soon, they were surrounded by ferocious wolves.

Suddenly, the Beast sprang from the shadows. He fought off the wolves until Belle was safe. But the Beast had been injured.

Belle returned to the castle to help nurse the Beast's wounds.

"If you hadn't run away, this wouldn't have happened," he complained.

"If you hadn't frightened me, I wouldn't have run away," Belle replied. Then she added, "Thank you for saving my life."

"You're welcome," the Beast said quietly.

As the days passed, Belle began to see a different Beast. He was learning to be gentle and kind. Even little birds noticed the difference in him, perching on his shoulders and eating birdseed from his paws.

Everyone at the castle watched Belle and the Beast with hope. It seemed
as if the pair were beginning to care for one another. Maybe – just maybe –
the spell would finally be broken, and everyone would become human again.

One evening, after an elegant dinner, Belle and the Beast danced together. The Beast gazed at Belle. He wondered if he would ever find the courage to tell Belle that he loved her.

The Beast knew how much Belle missed Maurice.
He showed her a magic mirror, revealing an image
of her father lost and trembling with cold as he
desperately searched for her.

Sadly, the Beast released Belle from her promise and let her return
home to her father. He gave Belle the mirror to remember him by.
With only one petal left on the enchanted rose, it seemed that any
hope of breaking the spell was gone forever.

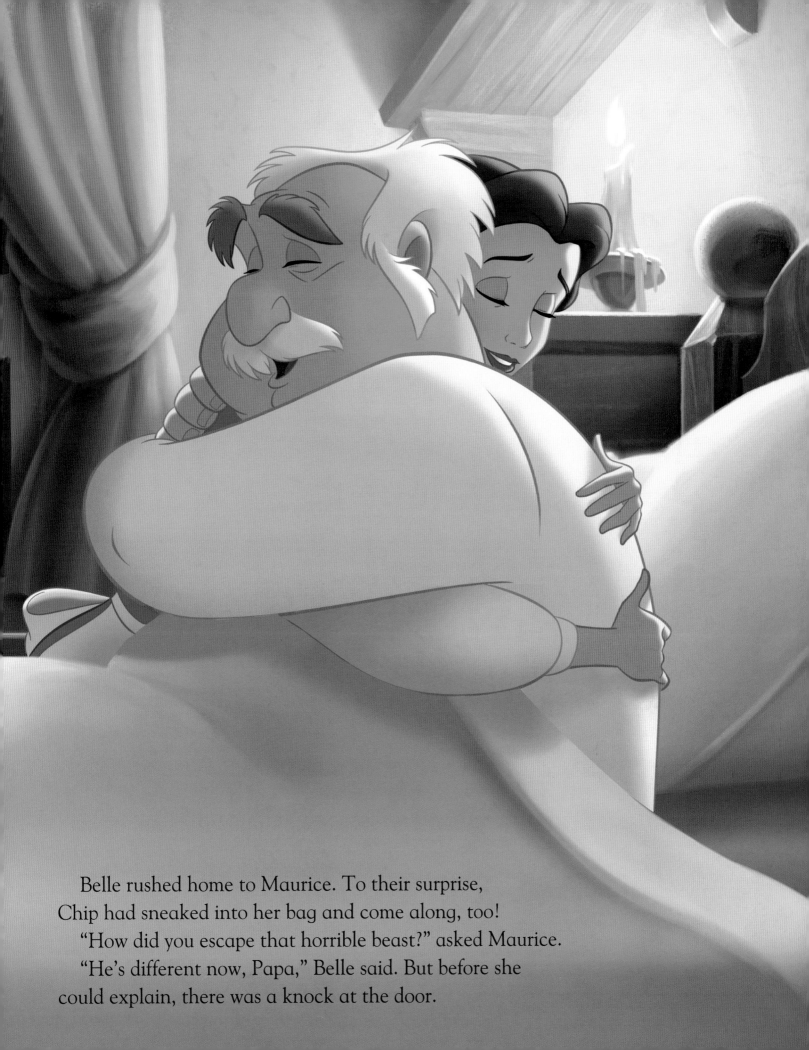

Belle rushed home to Maurice. To their surprise,
Chip had sneaked into her bag and come along, too!
  "How did you escape that horrible beast?" asked Maurice.
  "He's different now, Papa," Belle said. But before she
could explain, there was a knock at the door.

Gaston had bribed the owner of an asylum to declare Belle's father insane.
Maurice would be locked up in the asylum – unless Belle agreed to marry Gaston!
    As the guards dragged Maurice away, Gaston cornered Belle. "I might be able
to clear up this little misunderstanding," he said slyly, "if you marry me."
    "Never!" replied Belle.

To prove that her father wasn't crazy, Belle showed
people the Beast's image in the magic mirror. "He's my
friend," she told them.

Jealous and enraged, Gaston seized the mirror.
"Kill the Beast!" he shouted.

Gaston locked Belle and Maurice in their cottage.
Then he led a band of angry men to the castle.

With Belle gone, the Beast no longer cared about anything. "Just let them come," he said.

The servants tried to think of a plan.

When the angry mob stormed inside, the servants were ready! They fought and chased until the men ran away. Only Gaston remained.

Finding the Beast alone, Gaston raised his bow. When the arrow hit him, the Beast staggered back, crashing through the window and onto the castle roof.

Gaston followed the Beast outside and raised a club.
Before he could strike, Belle screamed out from below,
"No!" She and Maurice had escaped from the cottage
and raced to the castle.

Startled, Gaston paused. The Beast heard Belle's
voice, too, and was filled with hope. He suddenly found
the strength to defend himself.

The Beast lunged at Gaston then decided to let him go.
He climbed over to a terrace, where Belle had run to meet him.
All of a sudden, Gaston stabbed the Beast. The Beast roared
with pain and whipped around, accidentally knocking Gaston
off the roof! Gaston plunged through the darkness as he fell to
his death.

Belle pulled the Beast to safety and knelt beside him. "You came back," he whispered. "At least I got to see you one last time."

"Please don't leave me," Belle sobbed. "I love you."

As Belle spoke, the last rose petal fell.
Then, out of nowhere, magical sparkles
began to swirl around the Beast. He rose
into the air, turning slowly in a shower
of light. Belle watched in disbelief as the
Beast began to transform.

Magic swirled above the castle as
the servants were transformed, too.
The spell was broken!

"Belle!" cried the handsome prince.
"It's me!"

Belle gazed into the prince's eyes.
"It really is you!" she said in wonder.

Later, the servants watched as Belle and her prince waltzed across the ballroom.

"Are they going to live happily ever after?" Chip asked his mother.

"Of course, my dear," Mrs Potts replied. And so they did.